GARY GOPHER THE LAZY LOAFER

Kara Waller

Illustrated by
Sharyn Norton

GARY GOPHER
THE LAZY LOAFER

Kara Waller

Illustrated by
Sharyn Norton

Dedication Page

I dedicate this book to my son, Nathan for all the amazing things you are and have brought into our lives. We love escaping to the world of books together and seeing how the many different characters ignite your imagination.

Your curiosity has given a renewed wonder in the world, and I feel honored to see everything through your eyes.

To Mimi, who illustrated all these characters so that they can live in your imagination forever and so you will always know how loved you are.

About Author

Kara Waller has worked for 25 years in the media industry as an award-winning creative television producer, writer, and director. She has an amazing son and husband with whom she spends most of her free time, going to parks, biking, family trips to the waterpark, and building forts. Her son loves books and has quite a collection. He immerses himself in every page of a book, gets to know the characters, asks questions and makes up stories of his own. Kara worked on this book with her mother Sharyn, who did all the illustrations. Sharyn is an artist, who sketched and created the characters of Gophers Grove and most recently is working in oil paintings. The Picture Book is colorfully illustrated making it interactive for young children to follow Gary as he journeys on his quest of discovery.

As a child Kara loved her visits to the ranch where her grandparents lived in Texas. The cattle, the wide-open spaces and all the experiences that a ranch could provide. She was mainly captivated by her grandfather's biggest antagonist on the ranch, the gopher. Kara did not consider them to be the tunnel burrowing, plant eating little critters like her grandpa. Her fascination with the gopher community took on a much different perspective: A fantasy world where there was one gopher who didn't work as hard as the rest and comes to life in Gary Gopher the Lazy Loafer.

Life in Gophers Grove was much like any other town
Everyone was up at the break of dawn husslen' and busslen' around.

The Mayor, Gunther Goodfrey stood in the town square
rehearsing his speech for the Gophers Grove Fair.

The Schoolteacher, Grace Granville rang the school bell
as children gathered in the school yard with new stories to tell.

Grover the grocer opened his store for the day, while telling his wife
it is a beautiful morn in May!

Alarm clocks were going off all around,
awakening everyone to their day's duties in the town.

Everyone was busy and had something to do from firemen, bakers, to
keepers in the zoo.

ZOO
BAKERY
SCHOOL
FIRE DEPT
GG FD
GROCERY
GOPHERS GROVE FAIR
MAYOR
MAIL
SALE
Potato

In a corner of Gophers Grove where the meadows do run, lives Gill, Gloria and their three sons.

Gary's family went to work every day, but Gary would rather stay home and play.

Work was something Gary did not understand.
He wondered why this thing controlled everyone in the land.

"Mother, Father", Gary shouted, "We're being controlled." "Everyone is doing this thing called work until the day they grow old!"

TOOLS

Gary's father said, "Yes and it's time that you did too.
Your family and I work so why can't you?"

Gary said with a yawn, "It's just soooo boring mowing the lawn."

Gary's mother said, "You are becoming the biggest loafer in town.
Go find what you'd like to do without another frown!"

Gary obeyed and left looking sad and glum.
"Wait, I know who can help with this problem!"

LIBRARY

Gary went to see Gretta who works in the library.
"Hi Gary, is there a book you want to see?"

"No, Gretta, I don't need a book.
I need a job and I don't know where to look."

"What do you want to do Gary, do you know?"
He said, "I don't want to lift things, answer phones, or shovel snow."

"Do you have an interest that catches your eye?" He said, "I know I don't want to clean, build, or make pies."

"What is it Gary that you want to do?" "I don't want to sell things, fix things, or teach Kung Fu."

Gretta had an idea and said, "Ask everyone in the town why they do their work every day and this will help you find a job without delay."

"That's a great idea Gretta" Gary said with a snap "and it shouldn't even interfere with my 3:15 nap!"

SCHOOL
BUILD
FLOWERS
DOCTOR
TRAINS
X Y Z
WHERE
WHAT
HOW
A
B
C
DENTIST
SEW
WHO
cook
AIRPLANES
1+1=2
WORK
OOO
FIND JOBS
?
XXXX
MAKE
GROW
TEACHER
A
HOW TO
B
BAKER
PILOT
C
D
music
SCIENCE
E
HOW TO SELL $
FARMER
F
JOBS
DOGS TRAINER
G
XX
A-Z
Kung Fu
?
HOW TO FIX
HELP
GOPHER PEDIA
X
LAW
Z
HOW TO

Gary headed toward the town's grocery store
and Grover the grocer welcomed him at the door.

"Hi Gary," said Grover, "What can I do for you today?"
 "I want to know why you do your job every day?"

Grover said, "I do my job so everyone can have what they need, to help
others is my main job indeed."

Gary said "Thank You!" and walked on down the lane. He stopped in the
station to see Gus who runs the train.

They said their hellos and Gary asked Gus why he does his job every
day. Gus said, "So everyone can get to where they need to go in the best
possible way."

Gary left the station and walked to the Town Hall down the street. The
Mayor Gunther Goodfrey was who he was going to meet.

GROCERY
OPEN
SALE
APPLES
5¢
RAIL
CROSSING
ROAD
R R
GROVER
GROCER
GOPHERS
GROVE

Gary knocked on the mayor's door and walked right in. The mayor said, "Hello Gary, how have you been?"

"Fine Mayor, but there's something I'm trying to find out today. Why is it that people do their jobs every day?"

The mayor said, "Why that's simple Gary, everyone does their work so others can live. It is easy to take, but most like to give."

Gary said, "That's very true, I don't know why I didn't see it before." He thanked the Mayor and rushed out the door.

GOPHERS
GROVE
FAIR
SEPTEMBER
7

MAYOR

Gary ran and ran without any rest.
He ran across the town to the Daily Press.

Gary shouted, "Listen, Listen, I have something to say, I've learned of great news on this very day!"

Goodwin the Editor, said "What is it Gary that you would like to say? Gary said, "I would like to write of what I've learned today!"

"This news is wonderful and special and great! I have to write it down because I can no longer wait!"

GAZETTE
GAZETTE
Certificate
of
Achievement
GOPHERS GROVE
GAZETTE
WORK IS GREAT
WORK IS GREAT
WORK IS GREAT
NEWS
INK
NEWS
GAZETTE

Gary's article was in the next Gophers Grove Gazette and everyone was pleased with what their eyes met!

GOPHERS GROVE GAZETTE

THE WORLDS FAVORITE NEWSPAPER

An Article by **Gary Gopher**

Everyone of Gophers Grove, I have learned something new.
Something that is good for the many and the few.

I've learned of work and why it is done.
I now know that work is helpful and fun.

Jobs are done so that it is easier for everyone to live, and this why others work and give.

All of Gophers Grove was very happy with what Gary wrote in the Gazette. Everyone said that it was one of the best papers yet.

Gary's job was to write for the newspaper every day and the whole town couldn't wait to read what he had to say!

WE'RE PROUD OF YOU GARY
Work is Great !
GARY
GG FD
GG
MAYOR
TOOLS

How would you help Gary find a job ?

What would it be?

What is your favorite book?

Who is your favorite character in the book?

What job would you like to do when you grow up?

What is your favorite thing to do just for fun?

www.ingramcontent.com/pod-product-compliance
Lightning Source LLC
Chambersburg PA
CBHW041345300726

48978CB00005B/147